Wicked Widows' League

Wicked Widows' League

WICKED WIDOWS' LEAGUE
BOOK ONE

DAWN BROWER

"...when pain is over, the remembrance of it often becomes a pleasure."

— **JANE AUSTEN, PERSUASION**

Contents

Prologue	1
Chapter 1	5
Chapter 2	13
Chapter 3	20
Chapter 4	26
Chapter 5	33
Chapter 6	41
Chapter 7	47
Epilogue	55
Thank You	59

EXCERPT: HER ROGUE FOR ONE NIGHT

Prologue	63
Wicked Widows' Books	69
Acknowledgments	71
About Dawn Brower	73
Also by Dawn Brower	75

This is a work of fiction. Names, characters, places, and incidents are products of the author's imagination or are used fictitiously and are not to be construed as real. Any resemblance to actual locales, organizations, or persons, living or dead, is entirely coincidental.

Wicked Widows' League © 2022 Dawn Brower

Cover art by Mandy Koehler Designs

All rights reserved. No part of this book may be used or reproduced electronically or in print without written permission, except in the case of brief quotations embodied in reviews.

For all those that find strength when they need it most. Do not give up. You never know what you might discover in the middle of your journey.

Prologue

Katherine Lockley, the Countess of Wyndam lowered herself into a chair in the sitting room at the dower house she resided in. A fire had been lit in the hearth, but a chill remained in the room. She could feel the frigidity in her bones. As the years passed by, the more her body rebelled against her. Her knees failed her often forcing her to use a cane. She stared down at the offending accessory she wished she didn't need and frowned. Her grandson, Hudson Lockley, the current Earl of Wyndam had gifted it to her when it had become obvious, she would need one. It was mahogany and had carvings of large wild cats etched into the side. The handle had a sizeable sapphire at the top—Hudson claimed it matched her eyes—the charming scoundrel lied, but she'd allowed it. Her eyes had never been that vibrant blue, but his words had made her smile, nonetheless. Katherine had to admit she found the cane lovely to look at. That had probably been her grandson's plan all along.

Cheeky rogue that he was…

She had difficulty telling him no. He was the only family she had left. Katherine would do anything for him and had over the years. She wouldn't be around forever, and she worried about him. He needed more in his life, but he showed no signs of settling down.

Katherine glanced at her cane. She'd been alone a lot of years. Most of them had been by choice, but there was a time she'd been in love and thought nothing could ever happen to destroy that. She'd been mistaken—young, naïve fool that she'd been. Katherine had been wrong on a lot of things; however, there had been one thing she'd done right.

The league…

Her widows were her legacy. Katherine smiled, leaned back, and closed her eyes. They hadn't always been a part of her life. She had plans for this new set of widows. They didn't know it yet, but they would continue her legacy.

For now though, she wanted to reminisce—travel through her memories and revisit her past. When she was younger, her brown hair hadn't been streaked with gray, her blue eyes weren't faded, and her bones didn't ache. Her angular face and sharp cheekbones certainly had not been weathered with wrinkles...

It had been a different time and those experiences had led her to the person she'd become…

One

Many years earlier…

Katherine paced outside her husband's chamber. The doctor had been inside forever. Hours and hours and still no word… Did men feel this way when they waited for their wives to deliver a baby? At least that usually led to a happier outcome. This? Nothing could compare to waiting to be told if her husband would live or die.

He couldn't die. He just couldn't…

Not now when they finally had a son. It had taken months for her to conceive and when she had…they'd both been so happy. Their son, William, hadn't even reached his first birthday. In a few short months he would be a year old, and she prayed he would have many more years after that.

Their son couldn't grow up without a father.

Katherine refused to believe her husband would die. There had to be something the doctor could do to help Richard. His sickness had progressed until he could barely breathe. He gargled every time he drew a breath. It echoed through the room, and she barely suppressed a flinch with each intake of air. Richard's skin had lost all color. He looked close to death.

The door creaked open, and the doctor stepped out. He closed the door behind him. Katherine rushed to his side. "How is he?"

The doctor shook his head. "It's not good news."

Her heart sank. She feared he wouldn't survive, but hope was a hard thing to kill. "There's nothing you can do?"

"I'm afraid not. His illness has overtaken his body. It's only a matter of time before he takes his last breath." The doctor had a solemn expression on his reddened face. His hair had gone white, and his eyebrows were bushy, almost overtaking his forehead.

She couldn't look directly at him, or she'd laugh

maniacally—the absurdity and devastation overwhelmed her. Katherine had to remain calm. Her husband depended on her. "I can't believe that. There has to…"

"There isn't," the doctor interrupted her. "I have seen too many people with this illness. Anything that could be done has, and now we can only wait and make him as comfortable as possible."

"Until he dies…" She swallowed hard. Tears threatened to fall but somehow she managed to keep them inside. Crying wouldn't give her husband what he needed. Richard needed a miracle, and the doctor didn't have one to give him. "He's too young to die."

"Death knows no age," the doctor replied in a grave tone. "You need to prepare yourself."

Katherine wanted so to smack him. He was speaking the truth, but that didn't men he had to be so callous about it. He threw out epithets and dictates as if she were unaware of the realities of the world. Her husband was dying. Of course she didn't want to believe it. What she'd said hadn't been wrong. Richard was far too young to be dying on her now. She didn't need the doctor to remind her that death was in inevitability and a person could succumb to it at any stage of their life. Katherine would not cry though. She probably would later, but now she had to stay strong. Especially in front of the doctor… "How much time does he have?"

"Hours at most," he said. "I've given him something to help him rest. You can go in and be with him."

She nodded. "Very well. I trust you can see yourself out." Katherine didn't want to see his face any longer. He had to go, and the sooner the better. Her husband needed her, but clearly not the doctor. His care wouldn't save Richard.

"I should stay…" The doctor sputtered out the words. He sounded offended she told him to leave.

"You said there is nothing you could do for my husband, or did I misunderstand you?" She lifted a brow.

"No, you did not. But…" The doctor had a confounded expression on his face.

He was probably unaccustomed to being tossed out of a sick person's home. It was likely he had never had a woman do so either. Good. She hoped he remembered this day for the rest of his life. Katherine certainly would.

"Then there is no reason for you to stay," she

interrupted him. A weariness settled inside her along with acceptance. The truth was difficult to acknowledge, but Katherine had no choice. "I can take care of my husband for what little time he has left. Good day, doctor."

She didn't wait for him to say anything else, and she presumed he would find his way out of the house. What use was a doctor that couldn't save a person's life? Katherine opened the door to her husband's chamber and entered. She left the door open. There was no reason to hide her husband's condition. He was dying. She might not like that fact, but she had to accept it. Denial would not do anyone any good.

"Richard." Her voice was soft and firm as she spoke. She wanted to give in to her emotions and break down. To let all her pain and anguish flood out of her. Seeing him so broken down destroyed a part of her. Katherine's beautiful, warm, loving husband was a shell of the man she'd married. She hated feeling so damn helpless. "I'm here," she said. Her voice was a little hoarse now. Nothing could be done about that.

Richard opened his eyes. "Katie," he said. "I don't want to leave you."

If he kept saying things like that she'd definitely

break down. "I know you don't." She cupped his cheek in her palm. "I love you."

"Love you more," he choked out, then started coughing. She grabbed a nearby cloth and held it to his mouth as blood slid over his lips. Her heart beat heavily inside her chest. He wheezed in a breath. "I'm so sorry darling." He coughed again and it sounded even worse. Katherine hadn't thought that was possible. Her stomach sank as his breaths became even more ragged. Each wheeze was a stab to her heart. "I don't want to die. I'm a terrible husband for leaving you." Richard closed his eyes and struggled to breathe. "I've failed you."

"You have done nothing of the sort," she chastised him. Katherine couldn't let him die thinking she blamed him for becoming ill. Richard couldn't have prevented this. "You have been the best husband. I've been lucky to have you in my life. Don't ever believe I think less of you."

"I think less of myself." He struggled to get the words out. "Tell William I loved him. Help him know me." Richard struggled to speak each word.

She struggled to hold in the tears. "He won't ever doubt that you adored him."

He nodded. "Good." Something in his eyes had

changed. Richard seemed to look right through her. Almost as if he finally had accepted his fate.

"You should rest. This isn't helping you." She wanted to hold him in her arms and protect him from what was to come.

"There's no helping me." He met her gaze. "You have to promise me something." His breathing had a rattling sound now with each intake of air.

"I'll try," she said. Katherine didn't want to make a promise she might not be able to keep. What if he asked too much from her? Watching him struggle to breathe was difficult enough.

"Don't close your heart," he said. His tone was firm even though he had difficulty speaking.

"I am..." How dare he ask that of her? "I can't..."

"You can," he insisted. "Don't be one of those bitter widows. Let yourself love again. If not for yourself, or even me, but for our son... He should see what love is."

"All I can promise is that I won't push it away if it presents itself," she conceded. Katherine would never marry again. She didn't have any intention of allowing another man to have her heart. "But I don't know if I can pursue it again." It hurt too much when it was yanked away…

"That will have to be enough then," he told her. There was a finality in his words. Katherine's breath hitched and her lips trembled from the effort to hold back her tears.

Richard closed his eyes and took one final breath. The doctor had been wrong about the length of time her husband had left, but not the conclusion. Richard had died, and somehow Katherine would have to move forward.

Two

Three months later…

Could there be any worse color than black? Especially when Katherine's mood remained solemn. The weather hadn't helped either. The skies had been gray and gloomy for days. At least her outer appearance matched everything surrounding her. She'd have to become accustomed to wearing the dreaded color though. It would be all her wardrobe consisted of for many more months to come.

"My lady, pardon the interruption…" Her lady's maid stood in the doorway to Katherine's bedchamber. She rang her hands together in a desperate fashion. All the servants were nervous around her since Richard's death. They didn't seem to know what to do or say to her anymore.

"What is it, Mary?" she asked. She hadn't treated any of them differently. Her sadness must be permeating the air around the house. She would have to try to set it aside. It wasn't good to have so much melancholy in one household, and she didn't want to do anything that might be detrimental to her own son's wellbeing either.

"Your solicitor is here," she told Katherine. "He says it is important."

"It usually is when your solicitor pays you a call," Katherine replied dryly, then sighed. "Take him to my sitting room and order tea. I'll be down in a few moments." She needed a few more minutes to prepare herself for the solicitor. Since Richard's death she'd had more estate matters to handle than she could ever have anticipated. What could the solicitor want now? Hadn't they settled everything?

She took a deep, fortifying breath, smoothed down her black skirts, and then strolled out of her room. It didn't take her long to reach the sitting room. The solicitor was already seated and looking out the window when she entered. "Mr. Collins," she greeted him and then pasted a smile on her face. Reasons to smile were few and far between these days… "To what do I owe the pleasure of your visit?"

"Lady Wyndam." He bowed. The solicitor was always serious and never bothered with small talk. This visit should be no different. "My apologies for coming by unannounced but it couldn't be helped."

She nodded. "I trust this reason is of the upmost importance then?" Katherine lifted a brow. "What has happened?"

"There is an addendum to your late husband's will that has only just now been brought to light." Mr. Collins' expression was grave. Drat. That couldn't be good.

"What pray tell did my husband add that has you so concerned?" Richard wouldn't do anything that would harm her or their son. What did this addendum contain?

"It concerns your son," Mr. Collins said flatly. Katherine's heart beat heavily inside her chest. What about William? "After his birth your husband decided provisions should be made in the event of his death."

This didn't surprise her. Richard had planned as much as he could for any possibility. After William had been born, he'd probably considered everything that could happen. It was a practical thing to consider. This provision couldn't be a terrible thing. Right? "What were my husband's wishes?" She hoped she wasn't incorrect in her assumptions. She had to believe her husband meant only the best of intentions. Richard had loved her and their son. He would have only wanted what was best for them.

"He has appointed a guardian for the young earl until he reaches his majority." Mr. Collins cleared his throat. "He is to oversee everything. Even your personal inheritance."

Katherine couldn't hold in the gasp. Why would Richard have done such a thing? She didn't need a man to oversee her. She might understand more if he'd only appointed a guardian for William. Having a male presence in her son's life should be beneficial. Especially, since William's father had died before he reached his first birthday; however, that did not mean she appreciated having a man she did not know have a say in her life. "Why is this only coming to light now?" She needed all the information. Katherine would not react until she understood everything. Her first instinct was to act like a shrew and refuse to allow the appointed guardian in her home. It would be a futile effort of course, but the fit of rage might feel good.

"The office has been in a bit of chaos of late,"

Mr. Collins began. "One of our associates retired and organizing has been a bit...difficult. He wasn't as diligent about keeping his records in one place." Mr. Collins took a deep breath. He met her gaze and continued, "He's the one that had written the addendum for the late earl. One of our clerks found it earlier today. I came to see you straight away after I realized its significance."

"Is the proposed guardian aware of this sacred duty? Is he up to the task of overseeing my son's estate?" Katherine asked. She didn't ask about her own circumstances. She had a voice and would use it if she needed to. "When can I expect him to insert his influence?" Because it had to be a man...a gentlemen of high rank... Her husband would have left her in charge of her own life if he believed a woman could make decisions for herself. How had she not known that about him? The betrayal coursing through her was profound. She would not overcome it anytime soon. "Who did my husband choose to appoint guardian of my son." *And me...*

"The Earl of Dryden," Mr. Collins told her. "I believe he went to school with your late husband, but I'm not certain." He waved his hand. "That's not important though. The earl is not currently in London. I will pay a call on him in a few days at

Dryden Abbey and discuss it with him. His estate is in Hampshire."

"What if he doesn't wish to take on this responsibility?" Katherine asked. She hoped he would refuse to be William's guardian, but she didn't know what would happen if he did.

"He's already agreed. His signature is also on the addendum acknowledging the late earl's wishes." Mr. Collins informed her. The serious expression on the solicitor's face hadn't wavered once since she'd entered the sitting room.

"And will I be privy to those details?" She feared the answer to that question, but she had to ask.

"Not all of them, my lady," he said. "Only the ones that directly affect you." The solicitor stood. "Now that I've informed you, I must go. There is much yet for me to do, and the day is growing late. Have a good day." He nodded at her.

The maid pushed in a cart of tea as the solicitor walked toward the door. Refreshments were no longer needed, and she had no appetite. Eating and drinking had become monotonous since Richard's death. She ate because she had to remain healthy for her son, but she'd lost some weight. Food meant nothing to her, and the tea would go to waste.

"Take the cart back to the kitchen, Sarah. Let the servants have it."

"My lady," Sarah said in a cajoling tone. "You should have some…"

"I will Later," Katherine said dismissively. "I promise." She added when Sarah didn't leave. "The solicitor's news was unsettling, and I have much to consider."

"Very well, my lady," Sarah said soothingly. "Do try to remember to have some sustenance today. We worry about you."

Katherine didn't respond to her or even lift her gaze to meet hers. Sarah meant well. All the servants did… But she didn't think they understood how difficult her loss was on her. The weight of her grief suffocated her, and now she had even more to contend with. How much was one person supposed to be burdened with without falling to pieces?

Sarah sighed and pushed the cart back out of the room. What would happen to them all with a man Katherine was barely acquainted with in charge of their lives? She had met the earl once, and he hadn't impressed her—Richard clearly trusted him though. She didn't know what her future would be, and she didn't like it. Not one bit…

Three

It had been a week since Mr. Collins dropped by unannounced and delivered unsettling news. She had yet to hear from Lord Dryden. Katherine wouldn't be able to fully relax until he did or said something to alleviate her concerns. Nothing would ever truly put her at ease. She hated the position Richard had put her in and she didn't know what she could do about any of it. Probably nothing… What options did she truly have? None. The law was not on her side, and she might as well face that fact and accept it.

She settled down onto a nearby chair and leaned her head back. Her head hurt and she hadn't been sleeping well—she rubbed her temple, hoping it would ease the ache. Sleep had been difficult since Richard's death and she didn't foresee that changing any time soon. The announcement that she would have to contend with a guardian not only for William, but herself, had only added to her inability to rest.

"My lady," the butler said from the entrance of the sitting room. "A Mr. Collins is here to see you."

Of course he would randomly appear again. As if his last visit hadn't left her in a constant state of unease. "Please show him to the sitting room and have tea brought in." Perhaps he would stay long enough to have a cup this time. Either way she needed the tea to soothe her.

"Lady Wyndam," Mr. Collins greeted her. He looked a little haggard as if he had been wearing the same outfit for a while. "Please pardon my interruption. I've been traveling for days and there is much we need to discuss." That explained his attire at least.

"Very well," she said in a polite tone but prepared herself for the worst. What else could he possibly say that would make a difference now? She already had what little freedom she had ripped away from her. "Please continue."

"It seems there was a minor mistake in the addendum to your husband's will," he began. He sat down in a chair near her. "The clerk that read it aloud to me didn't read the entire document. He's been dealt with, but that's not the issue here."

"And what pray tell is?" What else could Richard have done?

"Your husband only wanted Lord Dryden to have guardianship in the event you were incapable of doing so yourself. The bulk of the portion left to you remains under your supervision as long as you remain unmarried. There is a small portion that your son's guardian will see to, but that involves the dower house and its upkeep. Those funds will take care of that." He cleared his throat. "I assume, for now, you will want to remain in Wyndam Castle in Sussex or Wyndam House while in London until your son reaches his majority."

"You assume correctly," she replied. The relief that flooded her was as overwhelming as the anxiety had been. Katherine didn't know what to make of it. Of course Richard wouldn't have made her deal with a guardian for herself. He understood her. Not all women were as lucky as she had been. Most husbands wouldn't consider their wives' wishes. Katherine had a couple important questions before Mr. Collins departed. "Have you met with Lord Dryden?"

"I have," he told her. "He's making arrangements to travel to London and meet with you. Since your son is still so small, he'll have little to do with his daily care right now. As he grows, he'll discuss important things like his education. For now he will oversee your son's estate until he's old enough to take over that responsibility."

All of that made sense. She wouldn't like having to contend with her son's guardian, but she wouldn't be the first or the last widow with that hardship. "Very well," Katherine said. "When should I expect Lord Dryden's visit?"

"He will be here in a fortnight. There were a few estate matters he had to finish before he could travel to London." Mr. Collins stood. "If you have any questions, please let me know and I'll do my best to answer them."

"Thank you, Mr. Collins." The maid pushed in the teacart. "Won't you consider staying for tea?"

"I wish I could," he told her. The solicitor looked tired. His wig was askew showing his drab brown hair and there were dark spots under his eyes. "But I really must go. Have a good day, my lady." He nodded at her and then left the room."

Sarah brought the teacart over. "Would you like me to pour my lady?"

"Yes, please," she told the maid. Katherine glanced at the teacart and fought not to smile. "There's more than tea on that cart."

"Mrs. Higgins thought you might like something small to eat. She made your favorite sugar biscuits." Sarah handed her a cup of tea, then a plate with two biscuits on it.

Katherine smiled and took both. "Tell Mrs. Higgins I appreciate her thoughtfulness. I will enjoy these biscuits." She took a sip of her tea, and then nibbled on one of the biscuits. It was delicious. For the first time in a very long time she felt a sense of peace. At least until Lord Dryden made his appearance.

She didn't know much about the earl. Her husband had clearly trusted him. Katherine wasn't so ready to do the same. She liked to make her own decisions about a person. At least she had some autonomy in her life. "Sarah," she said to the maid. "I think I am going to go for a walk today. Can you tell Mary so she can help me prepare after I am done with tea?"

"Yes, my lady," Sarah said. She curtsied and then left Katherine alone. A lot had happened in a short period of time. Most of it was life altering. Today she would take back what little control she had left. She might be forced to wear black, then gray, then purple as she mourned her husband, but that didn't mean she had to close herself off entirely.

Katherine didn't much care what the ton thought of her. She fully intended to live her life as she pleased. Marriage had been wonderful, but she had no desire to attempt it again. She would remain alone. What she needed now were friends she could rely upon. Ones that she could talk to and help alleviate any loneliness that might sprinkle its way into her life.

But where would she find such ladies? Katherine feared that would be an impossibly, and she wasn't up to the task. At least not yet…

Four

Eighteen months later…

Katherine was grateful to be rid of all her black gowns. Her maid was in the process of packing them all away to be stored in the attic. Now that she was out of full mourning, she could wear some gowns with color. Of course those are various shades of light purple…but still some color. She hoped she would never have to wear such a dismal shade ever again.

"Are you sure you wish for these to be stored in the attic?" Mary asked. "There's little chance you'll ever wear them again."

"Especially as I intend to never marry again…" Katherine sighed. "I doubt anyone else will find them useful. I don't know what else to do with them. For now, the attic is the best place for them." She could always figure out what to do with them later. Katherine was just glad to have them out of her wardrobe.

"Very well, my lady," Mary said. "I must say it's nice to see you smile more."

The pain eased over time. The loss of her husband had devastated her, and a part of her would always carry that pain. Over time though, it had dulled to a low ache. She could breathe easier now and move past her agony. The only thing that gave her any grief these days was Lord Dryden. "It's nice to not be wallowing in misery." Katherine smiled.

"My lady," Sarah said from the doorway. "My apologies for interrupting…"

"What is it," she asked the maid.

"Lord Dryden is here. He wishes to speak with you."

Katherine rolled her eyes. Since Lord Dryden had been informed of his guardianship over her son, he'd been a thorn in her side. He always showed up at her home without any notice and the arrogant arse didn't care if he inconvenienced her in any way. William was too small for him to be this actively involved in her son's life. "Show him to the sitting room and tell him that I will join him when I'm done here. I might be a while, but if he wished to return in a few hours, I'll have more time for him."

"All right." Sarah curtsied and left the room.

She didn't think Lord Dryden would go away easily. She half feared he'd come searching for her in the house. Hell, he might just do that. She wouldn't put it past him. That man had more audacity than any person should. He did whatever the hell he wanted and didn't make any apologies for it. She often wondered what it might be like to be a man and be able to do whatever she wanted. It must be nice.

"My lady," Sarah interrupted her thoughts.

She lifted a brow. "What is it now?"

"Lord Dryden says he'll wait for you and since you're so busy he'll stay for dinner."

She cursed under her breath. "I'd prefer he doesn't, but I doubt I can persuade him against it now." Katherine shook her head. "Mary finish without me. You know what I want done and I trust you to pack everything away with care." There were more than the mourning gowns going up to the attic. Some of the items Richard had given her were being packed away too. Looking at them made her loss more acute. Maybe when a lot more time passed by, she could unpack them again.

Mary smiled. "I'll take care when packing it all away. Go visit with Lord Dryden."

"It won't be a pleasant visit," Katherine grumbled.

"He fancies you," Mary said. "That's why he visits so often. It has nothing to do with little William. It's you he desires."

Katherine's mouth fell open. "You're wrong." Lord Dryden didn't want her. Did he? She would never have considered it if Mary hadn't put the idea in her head. No. She had to be wrong. "He's William's guardian." If he did have feelings for her, it was good that he wasn't her guardian too. That would have made everything very awkward.

Mary shrugged. "I might be mistaken, but I don't believe so. When you speak with him observe how he is with you. Maybe you don't see if because you don't want that from him."

"Perhaps," Katherine muttered. "I'll consider what you suggested." With those words she left Mary to her task and went to the sitting room to visit with Lord Dryden.

It didn't take her long to reach the sitting room.

She found him leaning back against the settee drinking tea. He had foregone a wig and left his ash blond hair unpowdered. It was very unfashionable of him. Katherine hadn't worn a wig or powdered her hair in months, but that was because she rarely left the house. She kept her walks to her garden where no one witnessed her lack of fashionable attire. Why did he deign to leave his hair unencumbered?

"My lord," she greeted him. "My apologies for keeping you waiting. I've been busy with some household tasks."

"Nothing that requires my attention I presume," he said with a lifted brow.

"Unless you wish to oversee the packing of my widow attire, then no," she said in a cool tone. "I do not need your permission to pack anything in this household away and store it in the attic."

"Of course you don't but I wouldn't be doing my job if I didn't ask." His tone was like ice. "I hoped we could have a frank conversation, but it appears you're in a mood."

"I'm in a mood?" She glared at him. "What is that supposed to mean?"

He lifted his lips into a smile. It was probably supposed to appear charming, but it sent chills down her spine. Lord Dryden had a reason for dropping by so often, but she couldn't discern exactly what it was. Mary could be right, but Katherine didn't think it was so simple. "What can I do for you Lord Dryden? Did you come by for a reason?"

"I wish to discuss your son," Lord Dryden said.

"You do?" Katherine asked. "What pray tell would you like to know? He's almost two years old. He doesn't do anything you might find interesting."

"He'll need tutors soon," Lord Dryden began.

"Soon? Do you consider several years soon? He will have a governess long before he will need a tutor." This man was ridiculous. "What is the real reason you are here?"

His lips twitched. "You're no shrinking flower are you, Lady Wyndam?"

She had never been a shy wallflower if that is what he meant. Katherine spoke her mind. That was one of the attributes Richard had loved about her. "I don't see any reason not to be candid. I have no reason to hold my tongue."

"I know you're still in mourning," Lord Dryden began. "But I like you and I would like to court you."

She narrowed her gaze. "No." Mary had been

right, but she would not entertain Lord Dryden's suit.

"You won't even consider it?" Lord Dryden asked. He appeared a bit affronted by her refusal. Good. Katherine hoped it discouraged him.

"I will never marry again." She walked toward the doorway. "So there's no reason to consider anything, my lord. Now if you'll excuse me, I have much to do today. I've been informed you wished to stay for dinner. Please feel free to let the cook know. I won't be joining you." With those words she left Lord Dryden alone in the sitting room. She couldn't bear to spend any more time with him.

Five

Ten years later…

Katherine sat in the study going over the household accounts. As the years went by Lord Dryden left that duty to her. He did keep trying to court her, but she had managed to keep him at a distance. She wished the man would give up and find himself another woman to ask to be his wife. Katherine had no desire to be another man's property.

A knock on the door caught her attention. She glanced up as Lord Dryden walked in. She inwardly groaned. Not much had changed in the last decade. She had grown older, maybe a little wiser, but Lord Dryden had remained the same. He continued to annoy her. A part of her would never forgive her late husband for his choice of guardian for their son. "Lord Dryden," Katherine greeted him. She should stand, but she refused. Anything she did that was remotely friendly only encouraged him. Hell, sometimes she thought he liked her rudeness too. "To what do I owe this visit?"

"I have come to discuss young William's education. He will need to go to school soon. Where needs to be decided before his thirteenth birthday." Lord Dryden strolled into the study and took the chair near her at the table.

"Am I to trust you would like my opinion on what school my son will attend?" She lifted a brow. He never asked for her thoughts. Lord Dryden could be quite arbitrary. He hadn't even allowed her opinion on the tutors he'd hired. "Or are you here to inform me of the school you have already enrolled William in?" She was willing to wager on the latter.

"I'm considering both Eton and Harrow," he answered her. "I would like Lord Wyndam to visit both schools. It might help me to decide if he's along with me."

She stopped writing in her ledger and glanced up at him. Katherine knew that she would have to be separated from her son when he was sent away to school, but she hadn't been apart from him since his birth. She already didn't trust Lord Dryden, and she had to be all right with him traveling with him to both Eton and Harrow? He'd be gone for weeks with all the traveling and a proper visit at each school. "What benefit will it be to have him visit with you? Will you take his wishes into consideration?"

"I always do," he said and almost sounded offended. "He's my main concern. Why wouldn't I take everything into consideration? It is his future."

Katherine had wondered if he meant what he said or if he was saying what she wanted to hear. "I would hope that you did, but as you don't consider my wishes important how am I to understand that you take a small boy's to be so?" She set her quill into the inkpot. With Lord Dryden there she wouldn't likely get any more done in the accounts. After he departed, she'd continue her work.

"Will you be difficult and argue with me taking the boy?" Lord Dryden ignored her last statement, and he wondered why she refused to consider his suit. He'd make a terrible husband.

"William needs to continue his education if he's to be a proper lord and oversee his estates. I do not object to his attending either Eton or Harrow. Both are reputable schools." She folded her hands in her lap. "However, his father did attend Eton. My son may wish to follow the same path. I only ask that if that is the case you allow it. A boy should be able to honor his father if he so desires."

"I have no objection to that," Lord Dryden said. "Now that we have that settled, I'll inform Lord Wyndam we're to depart at dawn. I'll instruct a maid to prepare him for traveling."

He didn't give Katherine time to argue or respond to that statement. He was out of the room before she had a chance to consider his words. Drat. That man was the bane of her life.

William had been gone with Lord Dryden for a fortnight. Katherine was lonely. Her son didn't spend a lot of time with her, but they did have an hour or two a day where they were together. With him gone she felt the impact of his absence so acutely. To help with that loneliness she started taking walks with Mary in Hyde Park. So she wouldn't have to bother with a wig she kept her hair covered. She hated wigs and thought them a silly fashion.

"My lady," Mary began. "Perhaps you should consider rejoining society. It's not healthy to keep yourself locked away in the house."

"We are not in the house now, are we?" She wouldn't know where to begin with society. She had made a conscious choice to remain distant from it. "Besides it isn't as easy as you seem to think. Invitations stopped being sent to me years ago." Once she had come out of mourning, she had received several. When she didn't attend anything after a while they had stopped. Besides she didn't really wish to attend social gatherings like she used to. She wanted something more meaningful.

"Lady Wyndam," a woman said from her left. Katherine turned toward her. "I thought that was you." She smiled and walked over to her. Three other women accompanied her. "It's been a while and it's so good to see you."

She had her hair covered too—though she recalled she had pale blonde hair. She wore a dark gray walking dress. The women with her also had the colors of widowhood on them, though one wore black and the other two a shade of purple. Katherine frowned and faced the woman who had addressed her, a friend from when she was a girl. It had been a while since she'd seen this woman. "Lady Covington," she greeted her. "My apologies for not coming over to speak with you. I'm afraid I'm often distracted and do not always notice those around me."

Lady Covington smiled warmly. Her hazel eyes seemed to brighten with a hint of joy. Was she glad to see Katherine? "I understand. It's hard being a widow, especially one as young as we all are," Lady Covington said.

They were all past the bloom of youth, but they were far from old women. Lady Covington had attended a finishing school with Katherine. They had been good friends then. "I am sorry to hear of your loss. I hadn't realized you had lost your husband." Katherine's husband had been gone for a while now. It would still be fresh for these four. "Are you all doing well?" She wasn't familiar with the other two ladies.

"I am," she told her. "Let me introduce you to my companions. This is Mrs. Williamson," Lady Covington introduced the one woman. Dark locks peeked out of her black hair covering. "Her husband was killed in battle. He was a lieutenant." Then she gestured to another woman. "This is

Lady Andover and Lady Sylvan. Their husbands were also killed in battle." She frowned. "Mine stupidly fell off his horse and broke his neck. He'd had too much to drink." Three men that died in battle…

"A loss is still a loss," Lady Andover said in a soft tone. She was so young. Even younger than Katherine had been when Richard had died. She had soft brown hair and gray eyes. "It doesn't hurt any less."

"My husband didn't bother with me unless he wanted something. His death was a blessing," Lady Sylvan said. Her hair was fiery red and she had light green eyes. "I can't grieve what is a relief to me. I cried when I got the news, but not because I'll miss him. The relief overtook me."

"You must excuse us," Mrs. Williamson said in a conspiratorial tone. "Some of us had wonderful marriages, and the others…"

"Had rotten husbands that we would rather celebrate their deaths than mourn them," Lady Sylvan finished for her.

Goodness…these four ladies were refreshing. "I don't suppose the four of you would be interested in joining me for tea?" Katherine asked. "I would love to speak with you more."

"That would be lovely," Lady Covington said. "We would be delighted to join you."

Katherine smiled. This was what she needed and once they were safely indoors, she had a proposal for them. Fate had led them to her, and she fully intended to take advantage of the gift she'd received.

Six

Two years later...

Katherine leaned back against her chair and stared at the ladies in her sitting room. They had become four of her closest friends. After that fateful day they'd met walking in Hyde Park they had met for tea at least once a week. They were all out of mourning now and considering rejoining society. Katherine still had no real desire to do so.

"I'm thinking of hosting a ball," Lady Sylvan said. "I'm a marchioness. The ton will come. You know they're all curious about me. Especially since I'm still young enough to take a husband."

"Do you wish to remarry?" Lady Andover

asked. "I've been considering what it is I want." She was the timidest of the five of them. "My marriage was all right. He didn't beat me or anything."

"But he didn't love you either did he?" Katherine kept her tone soft as she spoke. "Perhaps you shouldn't rush into anything yet. You're a widow and don't need to marry if you don't choose to. Enjoy that freedom for a while."

"Listen to Lady Wyndam," Lady Covington told her. "She's been a widow a lot longer than any of us. Her experience is invaluable."

Katherine sighed she didn't want any of them to look to her as an example of what they should do with their lives. She had adored her husband, but even he had failed her. There was something she had been meaning to discuss with them for some time now.

"We all need to do what is best for us," Katherine began. "Remarrying was never an option for us—or at least that is what we believe. I suppose that could change with the right man. However, there is something you do need to consider if you choose to give yourself to another man."

"What is that?" Mrs. Williamson asked.

"Your loss of freedom. Once we say vows our husbands own us." Katherine sipped her tea. "If love and trust is involved that isn't anything we need to worry about. But even a cherished husband can make mistakes." Hers certainly had. "We should plan for our future. Whether we remarry or not."

"That's not a terrible idea," Lady Sylvan said. "My husband was an arse. I'm in no hurry to marry ever again, but even I can make foolish decisions. What do you propose we do?"

"I'm not certain…" She frowned. "I was thinking we could create a society for widows. A safe haven for those that need it… We've all been burned in some way by men. Perhaps what we should do is some sort of foundation where we can pay our dues, and if one of our widows are ever in need…"

"Then we will be able to help them," Lady Andover finished. "That is brilliant."

"I'm not sure how we would go about setting it up," Katherine said. "I haven't had a chance to uncover what is involved."

"I would like to do that part," Lady Sylvan said. "My income is the largest. I will talk to my solicitor. We should have property as part of the foundation, and I have the perfect place for it."

"You do?" Katherine frowned. "Where?"

"It is outside of London," she began. "Far

enough away that we can have privacy, but close enough it is a short carriage ride into the city." Lady Sylvan grinned. "It used to be the house my husband used for his mistresses. It became mine upon his death." She leaned forward. "It wasn't entailed, and he left any property to me not entailed." Lady Sylvan shrugged. "It was part of my marriage settlement. My father wanted to ensure I would never be destitute. I can't think of a better use of the property."

"What about other widows?" Mrs. Williamson asked. "Do we invite them?"

Katherine frowned. "I don't think all widows should be automatically invited. We have to ensure they can be trusted with our secret."

"If any men discover what we have planned they might try to stop it or even ensure we are miserable." Lady Covington took a sip of her tea, then set the cup down. "Men like to control the women in their lives. They might not realize it, but they do it as their right. That is how they were taught. No man can ever know what we are doing here."

"Then we need rules," Katherine said. "Binding ones. Agreements that a widow must sign if they're to be a part of our league of widows."

Lady Andover smiled. "We will be more than a financial powerhouse. This will be a place a woman can feel safe, seek advice, and find a sense of purpose."

"Exactly," Katherine agreed. This is what she had been craving. She hadn't been able to discern what she wanted until she met these women. They had helped her find herself again. "Lady Sylvan is handling the financial aspect; I'll write the agreement and rules." She turned toward the other two ladies. "Mrs. Williamson and Lady Andover you two can inspect the property we are to use and have it properly cleaned, furnished, and staffed."

"This is going to be so much fun," Lady Sylvan said, then smiled. "After we have it all set up, we can start to meet with other widows and determine who should be invited." She frowned. "Should we limit membership into our league?"

"We might need to if there are too many prospects." Katherine furrowed her eyebrows. "They need to at least be able to pay our dues to be a part of the league. We can't accept everyone."

"What if someone pays their dues for them?" Mrs. Williamson asked. "Like a benefactor?"

"That will have to be disclosed before the widow is accepted," Lady Sylvan said. "Especially since every widow invited will have to be approved regardless. That will be one of the considerations. We want to remain financially stable and what happens if their benefactor can no longer support their needs?"

"I'll add that to our rules and agreement," Katherine added. "We want to ensure this goes as smoothly as possible. We will need to add a section regarding how we aid any widow in need. That can be part of how we assist them." She took a deep breath. "After I draw up the draft of both we will all go over it to confirm it is exactly what we all want."

"We all have our tasks to complete," Lady Andover said. She turned to Mrs. Williamson. "We can start on ours tomorrow. We will need to inspect the property first."

"I'll have everything you'll need delivered to you this evening," Lady Sylvan told them. "Let me know if I can help in any way."

They both nodded. "Then it's settled for now."

Katherine sighed. It was all starting to become real. She'd have her secret society of widows soon.

Seven

Ten years later...

Katherine sat in the sitting room of the dower house. It had been her residence since her son married a year and a half ago. Soon he would be a father. She had never been happier. Her son had chosen well for himself. His wife was a lovely woman. Her name was Rosemary, and she was the sweetest, kindest person Katherine had ever met. She would be a wonderful mother.

She sipped her tea and enjoyed the afternoon sunlight streaming through the widow. She frowned when she noticed a carriage coming down the drive. It seemed to be moving too fast. Something wasn't right. Katherine stood and rushed toward the door.

She flung it open and stepped outside. William hopped from the carriage. "Mother, you must come. The baby is coming early."

The baby wasn't due for another month. William must be so anxious, and poor Rosemary… She didn't think twice. Katherine hopped into the carriage and William followed behind her closing the door as he did so. He rapped his knuckles on the carriage and told the driver to go. "Have you sent for the doctor?"

He nodded. "He's already with Rose," William said. "But it's not going well."

His face didn't have much color in it. Katherine understood the terror of waiting. It had been over two decades, but the pain of losing Richard was still fresh. At least she no longer had to stomach Lord Dryden's visits and insistence they should wed any longer. The earl had given up years ago and finally married another woman. "I'll do whatever you need." She had always been there for him. Katherine wouldn't fail him now. Not when he needed her the most.

The dower house wasn't too far from the Wyndam estate. It took thirty minutes to reach the main house. Once the carriage came to a stop William hopped out and then assisted Katherine.

They both rushed inside. The sound of screams echoed down from the upstairs. Katherine had never heard anything like it in her life. She couldn't remember her own time in childbed to compare it to. Had she screamed as loudly?

"Stay here," Katherine said. "I'll go check on her and come back once I know more. It's not a man's place to be there during childbirth. She can't be concerned about your feelings. Rosemary needs all her strength to bring that babe safely into the world." And not die herself… She didn't add that part on though. Many women died giving birth. It was a risk a woman took, gladly most of the time.

She went up the stairs and to the bedchamber. Rosemary's sobs echoed through the room. "I can't do it. I can't…"

Katherine didn't stop to think, just went to Rosemary and grabbed her hand. "You can," she encouraged. "Your babe needs you to be strong."

"Listen to her," the doctor said. "It's not much longer now. One more push and the baby will be out."

Rosemary had almost no color on her face. She looked tired and weak. How long had she been laboring before William had come to fetch her? She nodded at the doctor, and she pushed when she was told. Not long after that a baby's squalling filled the room. The doctor took the babe and wrapped it in a sheet and handed it to Katherine. She didn't like the look the doctor gave her. He went back to Rosemary and frowned, then he came back to her. "Take the babe to his father. I'm going to do all I can for his wife, but it doesn't look good. There's too much blood."

Katherine nodded. She understood what the doctor hadn't said. Rosemary was unlikely to make it and he hoped the new baby would help William's grief. Her son was about to get some devastating news. The realization he would now have a son of his own might not be enough to help him through that grief. She prayed it was though. Katherine would never have wished a similar pain as she'd experienced on her own son, but at least she was equipped to help him with it.

Six months later...

KATHERINE WAS ONCE AGAIN WEARING BLACK. SHE hadn't commissioned new gowns. Instead she'd had her old ones removed from storage and had them redone. Most of them had been salvageable. The fashion was horribly out of date, but what did she care about fashion? Her son was dead. He'd drank too much and fallen off his horse. William hadn't been able to control his pain. His grief had been too much. Losing Rosemary had destroyed him. Katherine understood all of that; however, she was disappointed she couldn't help her only son.

She couldn't give into her own grief. As much as she wanted to break down, she would once again have to be strong. Her grandson needed her, and she wouldn't fail him as she had her son. Hudson would have a future. He wouldn't follow the same path that William or Richard had. He also wouldn't have a guardian the likes of Lord Dryden to contend with. William had entrusted his son's care to Katherine. At least her son had trusted her where her own husband had not.

"The widows are prepared to aid you with anything you need," Lady Sylvan said at her side. "Everyone has been notified."

"I appreciate it," Katherine replied, but her tone was emotionless. Perhaps in time she wouldn't feel so empty. "And if I need it, I won't turn it away." The league had been created for times like this one. The widows would rally behind her. She hadn't been one of the founding members to deny that aid now.

"Is there anything you need immediately?" Lady Covington asked.

Katherine shook her head. "Nothing." What she needed was her son back. She wouldn't voice that because it was an impossibility. That would be her grief talking. "Your companionship is enough."

"Do you wish to take up residence at Matron Manor?" Lady Andover asked. "I can have a room prepared for you and your grandson."

Katherine considered it. Going to Matron Manor might be wise, but she couldn't do it. "Not now," she told her. "I need to be here, but I might reconsider later." When she was free to let her emotions control her. "There's too much to be done to go anytime soon."

"I understand," Lady Andover said. "Mrs. Williamson is there now. She wanted to be here…"

"We all have our duties," Katherine interrupted. "The league is constantly evolving. Someone has to be there at all times." They took turns staying at Matron Manor. When it was Katherine's turn to be in charge, that was when she'd take Hudson and take up residence. Not a moment sooner…

"If you don't need anything…" Lady Covington said.

"I don't," Katherine interrupted. "I do appreciate it. All I need right now is some time alone. I'll be all right. I promise. This isn't my first time experiencing grief."

"It isn't the same…" Lady Sylvan sighed. "But we understand. Someone will check on you in a few days."

That was part of their rules. When there was a widow in need, they kept tabs on her. Whether she liked it or not… Katherine had agreed, but she had never thought she'd be one of those widows in need of that type of care. "I'll be here." She smiled but didn't feel it. "Now go."

The three of them each came over and hugged her before they left. Once she was by herself a lone tear slid down her cheek. A parent should never have to bury their child. Unfortunately, it happened far too often.

She would be all right though. The widows would be her rock, and Katherine would be Hudson's. Katherine had far more now than she had when Richard had died. She had lost so much over the years, but she had gained one thing that changed everything.

A league of widows... The *Wicked Widows* to be more precise, but that wasn't their official name. They liked the sound of it and laughed when they had discussed what to call themselves. One thing was certain though. The foundation that they had created years ago would continue to be beneficial to any widow who joined their league. Katherine would make sure it did for as long as she lived.

Epilogue

Present day...

Katherine stared down at her cane once again and smiled. When Hudson visited her again, she'd thank him for it. She hadn't when he first presented it to her. It had made her a little sore to admit she needed it. Her work as a founder of the widows' league was never done though, and she was expecting a potential new member to visit with her soon.

"Lady Wyndam," her companion, Miss Juliet Adams, said from the entrance to the sitting room. It was too bad Miss Adams wasn't a widow. She didn't meet the requirements to be part of the league, but Katherine had never met a woman more in need. At least she could help by hiring her to be her companion. "There is a Mrs. Claudine Grant here to see you?"

"Please show her in," Katherine said. "And Juliet…"

"Yes?" She lifted a brow. Her golden blond hair was twisted into a chignon and her blue eyes were sharp with hidden wit.

"Do leave us alone after you show her in. This is private business."

Juliet snorted. "As if I'm unaware of your little widows club." She waved her hand dismissively. "Don't worry I won't say anything. I'll leave you two alone."

Katherine didn't have to wait long. Juliet escorted Mrs. Grant into the room. She had rich brown hair and green eyes. In some ways she reminded Katherine of Mrs. Williamson. Her friend had died a year earlier, and she missed her. Like Mrs. Williamson, Mrs. Grant was the widow of a lieutenant. Both of their husband's had died in battle. "Come in, Mrs. Grant," Katherine encouraged. "There's much we need to discuss."

She walked over to Katherine and fidgeted. Mrs. Grant was so very young. It made her wonder if she had ever been like the youthful widow. How long had she been married before her husband had been taken from her? Katherine stomped her cane on the ground. "Sit and tell me your story?"

"My story?" She nearly stuttered those two words out. "I don't understand."

"Tell me how you came to marry your lieutenant," Katherine told her. "Then we can move on from there."

Mrs. Grant sat in the chair across from Katherine. "James was a handsome man." She smiled as she tilted her head to the side. The young widow was remembering their beginning. It was so nice to remember that part, especially if it had been good. Katherine understood that better than most. "He loved me so." Mrs. Grant twisted her fingers together. "I suppose I loved him too." She lifted her gaze to meet Katherine's. "Is it wrong to question that now?"

"No dear," she said in a soft tone. "It means you understand yourself. In that you're lucky. Not everyone as young as you are do."

This widow would be all right. She was also a good fit for the league. She would be a strong leader and some of the widows would be able to lean on her. Katherine nodded at her. "Finish your story."

Mrs. Grant began speaking again, and Katherine leaned back to listen to her tale.

It was time for a new generation to take over the league. She would find some good women to lead the widows. Starting with this Mrs. Grant. With her help Katherine's Wicked Widows would continue to be a secret league that helped these new widows be the women they were always meant to be. She couldn't wait to watch them find their paths, and soar…

Thank you so much for taking the time to read my book.

Your opinion matters!

Please take a moment to review this book on your favorite review site and share your opinion with fellow readers.

www.authordawnbrower.com

Excerpt: Her Rogue for One Night

WICKED WIDOWS' LEAGUE BOOK TWO

Prologue

Claudine Grant glanced up at the dark clouds in the sky. They were an omen of some sort. She had a feeling in her stomach that unsettled her, and had since she'd woken earlier that morning. That feeling of dread wouldn't go away, and as the day progressed it worsened.

Even if the clouds were not an omen of bad things to come they did alert her to one thing with certainty. A storm was brewing. She should go back inside, but she couldn't make her legs move.

She had a letter from her husband, James waiting for her inside. Claudine hadn't opened it yet. Letters from James rarely came. He was away at war fighting against Napoleon. It seemed like an endless war and she feared she would never see him again. What if this was the last letter she ever received from him?

They married one day before he left for war. Their marriage had been quick. Well, as quick as it could be done. The banns were read and after the third week they said their vows. They'd had one night together, and then he had to leave. Then she was alone in their small home. Claudine had two servants—a maid and a cook. James was the third son of a viscount. His commission had given him his rank and position. He was a lieutenant in the Calvary.

All Claudine wanted was for her husband to return to her. She should read his letter. She glanced up at the sky once more and headed home. It didn't take her long to reach the entrance. She went inside and to her writing desk. Claudine pulled out the letter and broke the seal. Folded inside the letter from James was another note. It only had her name scrawled across it. Her hands shook as she picked it up. It wasn't in James' handwriting. Who else would be sending her a letter?

She set it aside and ran her fingers over the

words James had written her. His handwriting was so familiar to her. She finished unfolding it and started to read it from the beginning.

My Dearest Claudine,

Today was a good day. There are not to many of those here. The sky was a brilliant blue and the sun bathed us in its light. The warmth felt wonderful against my skin. I wish I could have enjoyed it more. I wish I could have spent this day with you cradled in my arms.

This letter I'm writing out of necessity. These words should come from me. If the worst should happen… God I can't imagine the worst. Everyone should be able to live their lives with the freedom of not considering that possibility. As a soldier I am not so fortunate. If I had not chosen this life I would be with you.

But if that possibility should happen I don't want to leave anything unsaid. My wonderful, beautiful wife—I adore you. There are no words that can adequately describe how much I love you. The greatest day of my life was when you agreed to be my wife. Our wedding day will be forever honored in my memory. As far as regrets go, that is one thing that will not be tallied under that column. My heart will forever be yours. I will always belong to you, and only you.

My hope is that this letter will be fodder for a fire one day and you will never read it. That soon I'll be home and kissing you, loving you, and spending the rest of my days by your side. However, I must be pragmatic. If you are receiving this letter, then my love, I am no longer amongst the living. Confirmation will come from someone of authority, but for now, this will have to do.

Before I left I ensured that all my particulars were in order. You will be taken care of, and if you so choose you may remain in the home we selected together. If it doesn't suit you, sell it and find another. And my love…try to let me go. I want you to be happy.

All my love,
James

A tear fell down her cheek. She should have avoided reading the letter longer. She could have remained in blissful ignorance. This couldn't be real. James was not dead. Claudine refused to believe it. She picked up the other folded piece of paper. There was a quick note jotted down there. Almost as if an afterthought…

She needed to read the letter. Claudine's hands shook as she stared down at the parchment. The missive wasn't long. Perhaps that meant it wasn't the

EXCERPT: HER ROGUE FOR ONE NIGHT

news she feared? No. That possibility was unlikely. She had to read it and find out. All the supposition was not helping her.

Dear. Mrs. Grant,

I served with Lieutenant James Grant. He is…was an honorable man. He died in service to his country. You can be proud of the man he was and all that he did. His actions saved the lives of several men in our unit. Without him, there would be more men being mourned. I am sincerely sorry for your loss. Lieutenant Grant will be missed by us all.

Yours truly,
Colonel Andrew Roberts

This letter sounded far more official. She should visit James' father. Perhaps he knew more. She closed her eyes and held back the tears that threatened to fall. Now was not the time for giving in to tears. It was time to plan and get answers.

Claudine glanced out the window. The storm had rolled in. The sky had opened up and rain poured down. It beat against the window like a constant beat of a drum. The roads would be muddy in the morning making them nearly impassible. She would not let that fact stop her. This trip was too important. She'd pack and go to London in the morning. There she would visit the viscount and find the truth. Whatever that truth might be…

Order here:
www.books2read.com/RogueforOneNight

Wicked Widows' Books
RELEASE SCHEDULE AND ORDER LINKS

1. August 2022 **Dawn Brower—Wicked Widows' League**
2. March 21, 2023 **Dawn Brower—Her Rogue for One Night**
3. March 28, 2023 **Lana Williams—To Bargain with a Rogue**
4. April 4, 2023 **Cara Maxwell—Rogue Awakening**
5. April 11, 2023 **Ari Thatcher—My Lady Rake**
6. April 18, 2023 **Diana Bold—A Scoundrel in Gentleman's Clothing**
7. April 25, 2023 **Amanda Mariel—Rogue for the Taking**

8. May 2, 2023 **Courtney McCaskill—Scoundrel for Sale**
9. May 9, 2023 **Charlie Lane—Scandalizing the Scoundrel**
10. May 16, 2023 **Sue London—To Woo a Rake**
11. May 23, 2023 **Anna St. Claire—A Widow's Perfect Rogue**
12. May 30, 2023 **Rachel Ann Smith—Stealing a Scoundrel's Heart**
13. June 6, 2023 **Tracy Sumner—Kiss the Rake Hello**
14. June 13, 2023 **Nadine Millard—Seducing the Scoundrel**
15. June 20, 2023 **Jane Charles—Season of the Rake**
16. June 27, 2023 **Tabetha Waite—How to Choose the Perfect Scoundrel**
17. July 4, 2023 **Cecilia Rene—A Scandal with a Scoundrel**
18. July 11, 2023 **Shannon Gilmore—Kiss Me Like a Rogue**

Acknowledgments

Special thanks to Elizabeth Evans. Your encouragement and assistance with this book helped me immensely. I am grateful for all you do for me.

About Dawn Brower

USA TODAY Bestselling author, DAWN BROWER writes both historical and contemporary romance. There are always stories inside her head; she just never thought she could make them come to life. That creativity has finally found an outlet.

Growing up, she was the only girl out of six children. She raised two boys as a single mother; there is never a dull moment in her life. Reading books is her favorite hobby, and she loves all genres.

www.authordawnbrower.com
TikTok: @1DawnBrower

bookbub.com/authors/dawn-brower
facebook.com/1DawnBrower
twitter.com/1DawnBrower
instagram.com/1DawnBrower
goodreads.com/dawnbrower

Also by Dawn Brower

HISTORICAL

Stand alone:

Broken Pearl

A Wallflower's Christmas Kiss

A Gypsy's Christmas Kiss

Marsden Romances

A Flawed Jewel

A Crystal Angel

A Treasured Lily

A Sanguine Gem

A Hidden Ruby

A Discarded Pearl

Marsden Descendants

Rebellious Angel

Tempting An American Princess

How to Kiss a Debutante

Loving an America Spy

Linked Across Time

Saved by My Blackguard

Searching for My Rogue

Seduction of My Rake

Surrendering to My Spy

Spellbound by My Charmer

Stolen by My Knave

Separated from My Love

Scheming with My Duke

Secluded with My Hellion

Secrets of My Beloved

Spying on My Scoundrel

Shocked by My Vixen

Smitten with My Christmas Minx

Vision of Love

Enduring Legacy

The Legacy's Origin

Charming Her Rogue

Ever Beloved

Forever My Earl

Always My Viscount

Infinitely My Marquess

Eternally My Duke

Bluestockings Defying Rogues

When An Earl Turns Wicked

A Lady Hoyden's Secret

One Wicked Kiss

Earl In Trouble

All the Ladies Love Coventry

One Less Scandalous Earl

Confessions of a Hellion

The Vixen in Red

Lady Pear's Duke

Scandal Meets Love

Love Only Me (Amanda Mariel)

Find Me Love (Dawn Brower)

If It's Love (Amanda Mariel)

Odds of Love (Dawn Brower)

Believe In Love (Amanda Mariel)

Chance of Love (Dawn Brower)

Love and Holly (Amanda Mariel)

Love and Mistletoe (Dawn Brower

The Neverhartts

Never Defy a Vixen

Never Disregard a Wallflower

Never Dare a Hellion

Never Deceive a Bluestocking

Never Disrespect a Governess

Never Desire a Duke

CONTEMPORARY

Stand alone:

Deadly Benevolence

Snowflake Kisses

Kindred Lies

Sparkle City

Diamonds Don't Cry

Hooking a Firefly

Novak Springs

Cowgirl Fever

Dirty Proof

Unbridled Pursuit

Sensual Games

Christmas Temptation

Daring Love

Passion and Lies

Desire and Jealousy

Seduction and Betrayal

Begin Again

There You'll Be

Better as a Memory

Won't Let Go

Heart's Intent

One Heart to Give

Unveiled Hearts

Heart of the Moment

Kiss My Heart Goodbye

Heart in Waiting

Heart Lessons

A Heart Redeemed

Kismet Bay

Once Upon a Christmas

New Year Revelation

All Things Valentine

Luck At First Sight

Endless Summer Days

A Witch's Charm

All Out of Gratitude

Christmas Ever After

YOUNG ADULT FANTASY

Broken Curses

The Enchanted Princess

The Bespelled Knight

The Magical Hunt

Printed in Great Britain
by Amazon